THE LOST DRAGON RIDERS:FANTASY ADVENTURE DISCOVER THE SECRETS OF THEIR ANCIENT POWER

First edition. November 26, 2023.

ISBN: 979-8223517504

Written by Hadi hans.

TheLost DragonRiders

Summary

Chapter 1: A New Beginning

1. Sara's Frustration
2. The Hidden Cave
3. Zarok's Arrival

Chapter 2: Secrets of the Cloud-Cloaked Preserve

1. Journey to the Mountain
2. Meeting the Wizard Guardians
3. Elemental Dragon Riding Training

Chapter 3: Unveiling Danger

1. News of Dragon Poaching Threat
2. Daring Risks and Loyalty
3. The Gathering Storm

Chapter 4: Confronting Danger

1. Infiltrating the Poachers' Lair
2. Unexpected Allies
3. Showdown with Sinister Forces

Chapter 5: Triumph and Sacrifice

Chapter 1: A New Beginning

1. Sara's Frustration

Sara sat in the backseat of the car, her arms crossed tightly over her chest. She stared out the window, watching as the familiar cityscape faded away and was replaced by towering mountains and dense forests. Her family had moved to this remote mountain town for her dad's new research job, and she couldn't help but feel frustrated and annoyed.

She missed her friends, the ones she had known since kindergarten. They were like a second family to her, always there to laugh with or cry on their shoulders. Now, she was forced to leave them behind and start all over again in a place where she knew no one.

As they pulled up to their new house, Sara sighed heavily. It was a quaint little cottage nestled among the trees, far away from any neighbors or civilization. She hated feeling like an outsider in this strange new town.

1. The Hidden Cave

Determined to escape her frustrations for a while, Sara decided to explore the woods behind their house. Maybe she could find some solace in nature, away from the prying eyes of judgmental classmates.

As she ventured deeper into the forest, Sara stumbled upon a hidden cave tucked away beneath a cluster of ancient trees. Curiosity piqued, she cautiously entered the dark cavern.

Inside, she gasped at what she found—a glowing blue egg resting on a stone pedestal. Mysterious symbols were intricately carved into its surface, shimmering with an otherworldly light.

Sara's heart raced with excitement as she reached out to touch it gently. The egg felt warm against her fingertips as if it held some secret power within it.

1. Zarok's Arrival

That night, as Sara lay in bed unable to sleep, something extraordinary happened—the egg hatched right before her eyes! A crack appeared on its surface before it split open, revealing a baby dragon nestled inside. It was unlike anything she had ever seen before.

The dragon, who introduced himself as Zarok, emitted a soft glow that illuminated the room. Sara and her younger brother Noah watched in awe as the creature unfurled its wings and stretched out its tiny limbs.

To their surprise, Zarok formed an empathetic bond with both siblings. He spoke directly into their minds with a voice no one else could hear. He explained that centuries ago, a thriving dragon kingdom existed, but relentless dragon hunters drove his kind into hiding. Only a few hidden sanctuaries and bonded human allies remained.

Zarok needed their help to find his tribe and restore the balance of their magical world. Sara's frustration began to fade away as she realized the incredible adventure that lay ahead.

Interactions between Sara and secondary characters:

Sara's frustration was momentarily forgotten as she shared the news of their discovery with her family over breakfast the next morning. Her parents were skeptical at first but couldn't deny the magic emanating from Zarok.

Noah, her shy and nervous younger brother, was initially hesitant about this newfound responsibility. But seeing how excited Sara was about helping Zarok find his tribe, he mustered up the courage to join them on this extraordinary journey.

As they ventured deeper into the mountains alongside Zarok, they encountered wizard guardians who lived in harmony with dragons in a cloud-cloaked preserve. These wise beings taught Sara and Noah about their endangered magical world and trained them in elemental dragon riding skills.

Sara found solace in these interactions with the wizards and other young dragon riders who had also formed bonds with dragons like Zarok. They shared stories of bravery and friendship that inspired her to embrace her new role as a protector of this mystical realm.

Together, they formed an unlikely alliance—a society of magical creatures, human allies, and young dragon riders—dedicated to protecting the preservation lands from the looming threat of dragon poachers. Sara and Noah were determined to prove their loyalty and friendship as they faced daring risks to safeguard this hidden sanctuary.

With each passing day, Sara's frustration transformed into a fierce determination to make a difference in this magical world she had stumbled upon. Little did she know that this new beginning would not only change her life but also shape the destiny of dragons and humans alike.

(Note: The style of writing in this chapter is inspired by J.K. Rowling, with a focus on adventure, magic, and the power of friendship.)

7

Chapter 2: Secrets of the Cloud-Cloaked Preserve

1. Journey to the Mountain

Sara and Noah trudged up the steep mountain path, their breaths coming in ragged gasps as they struggled against the treacherous terrain. The wind howled around them, whipping their hair into a frenzy and making it difficult to see more than a few feet ahead. Sara's frustration grew with each step, her annoyance at being uprooted from her old life intensifying.

"I can't believe Dad dragged us all the way out here," she muttered under her breath, casting a resentful glance at Noah who was walking beside her, his face etched with nervousness.

Noah glanced up at his sister, his eyes wide with uncertainty. "I miss our old friends," he admitted softly.

Sara sighed, feeling a pang of guilt for not considering Noah's feelings earlier. "I know it's tough for you too," she said, reaching out to squeeze his hand reassuringly. "But maybe this place won't be so bad after all."

As they continued their ascent, the siblings stumbled upon an unexpected sight—a hidden cave nestled amidst the towering trees. Intrigued, they cautiously entered the dark cavern and were greeted by an ethereal glow emanating from within. Their eyes widened in awe as they discovered a glowing blue egg adorned with mysterious symbols carved into its surface.

1. Meeting the Wizard Guardians

That night, as Sara and Noah lay in their beds, they watched in astonishment as cracks began to form on the surface of the egg. With bated breaths, they witnessed its miraculous transformation—the hatching of a baby dragon right before their eyes.

The dragon emerged from its shell and immediately formed an empathetic bond with both Sara and Noah. In their minds, they heard its voice—a voice that no one else could hear—explaining the plight of its kind. Centuries ago, a thriving dragon kingdom had existed, but relentless dragon hunters had driven them into hiding. Only a few hidden sanctuaries and bonded human allies remained. The dragon fledgling, Zarok, needed their help to find his tribe.

Determined to assist Zarok and protect the dragons from further harm, Sara and Noah embarked on a journey up the mountain. With Zarok leading the way, they navigated through treacherous terrain and battled unpredictable weather. The wind whipped at their faces, threatening to push them off balance, while rain soaked their clothes and made the path slippery underfoot.

Finally, after what felt like an eternity of struggle, they reached the cloud- cloaked preserve—a sanctuary where dragons secretly lived alongside wizard guardians. As they stepped into the magical realm, Sara and Noah were greeted by a breathtaking sight—the sky above them was filled with majestic dragons soaring gracefully amidst billowing clouds.

1. Elemental Dragon Riding Training

The wizard guardians welcomed Sara and Noah with open arms, eager to share their knowledge of the endangered magical world that lay hidden within the preserve. They marveled at the beauty surrounding them—the lush greenery that stretched as far as the eye could see, punctuated by sparkling waterfalls cascading down rocky cliffs.

Under the guidance of experienced riders within the preserve, Sara and Noah began their training in elemental dragon riding skills. They were taught how to control their dragons' powers—fire for Sara's dragon and ice for Noah's

—and how to navigate through different terrains with grace and precision.

Days turned into weeks as they honed their skills, facing physical challenges that pushed them to their limits. They soared through narrow canyons with sheer walls towering on either side, feeling exhilaration course through their veins as they mastered each twist and turn. They learned to trust not only themselves but also their dragons—a bond forged through shared experiences and unwavering loyalty.

As they trained, Sara and Noah formed deep connections with their fellow riders and the wizard guardians. They listened to stories of past battles fought against the sinister forces that threatened the preservation lands. They learned about the importance of friendship, loyalty, and sacrifice in protecting their newfound home.

News soon reached them of a dangerous dragon poaching threat growing closer to their sanctuary. With hearts filled with determination, Sara and Noah joined forces with the society of magical creatures, human allies, and young dragon riders. Together, they embarked on daring missions to safeguard the preserve from those who sought to harm it.

With each adventure, Sara and Noah discovered the true meaning of loyalty and friendship. They faced danger head-on, relying on their newfound skills and the support of their companions. And as they fought to remove the threat looming over their beloved preserve, they realized that they were no longer outsiders—they were an integral part of a community bound by a shared purpose.

In this cloud-cloaked realm where dragons soared and wizards guarded secrets, Sara and Noah found not only a new home but also a sense of belonging that surpassed anything they had ever known before. And as they continued their journey alongside Zarok and their fellow protectors, they knew that together they would face whatever challenges lay ahead.

Note: This chapter is inspired by J.K. Rowling's writing style without explicitly mentioning her name.

12

Chapter 3: Unveiling Danger

1. News of Dragon Poaching Threat

The remote mountain town had become a sanctuary for Sara and Noah, where they discovered the hidden cave and the magical dragon egg. But their newfound peace was shattered when news broke about a dangerous dragon poaching threat growing closer to their sanctuary. The whispers spread like wildfire through the town, reaching Sara's ears as she walked through the school hallways.

Sara's heart raced with worry as she shared the news with Noah after school. "Noah, we have to do something," she said, her voice filled with determination.

Noah nodded, his eyes wide with fear. "But what can we do? We're just kids."

Sara placed a comforting hand on his shoulder. "We may be young, but we have Zarok by our side. And together with our allies, we can protect both dragons and humans from these sinister forces."

1. Daring Risks and Loyalty

With their newfound resolve, Sara and Noah joined forces with their allies to embark on daring missions to gather information about the dragon poachers. They ventured deep into the woods surrounding their mountain town, following leads and tracking down any signs of suspicious activity.

Their first mission took them to an abandoned warehouse on the outskirts of town. As they peered through a crack in the door, they witnessed the cruelty inflicted upon captured dragons. Tears welled up in Sara's eyes as she saw the pain etched on their scaly faces.

"We have to save them," Sara whispered fiercely.

Noah nodded solemnly beside her. "We can't let them suffer like this."

Their allies agreed, and together they devised a plan to free the captured dragons under cover of darkness. It was risky, but their loyalty to these majestic creatures fueled their determination.

As they crept through the shadows that night, adrenaline coursed through Sara's veins. She could feel the weight of responsibility on her shoulders, but she knew they were doing the right thing. The dragons deserved to be free.

1. The Gathering Storm

As the threat of the dragon poachers intensified, Sara and Noah's group faced their biggest challenge yet. They gathered in a hidden cave deep within the cloud-cloaked preserve, their faces etched with determination.

"We can't let them destroy our sanctuary," Sara declared, her voice filled with conviction.

Their allies nodded in agreement, their eyes reflecting a mix of fear and bravery. Together, they brainstormed ideas and devised a plan to confront the poachers head-on.

Days turned into nights as they prepared for the final showdown. They trained tirelessly, honing their skills in elemental dragon riding and strategizing every move. The bond between Sara, Noah, and Zarok grew stronger with each passing day, as if they were becoming one united force against evil.

Finally, the day arrived when they would face the poachers. The air crackled with tension as they made their way towards the heart of danger. Their hearts pounded in unison as they approached a clearing where the poachers had set up camp.

Sara's hand tightened around Zarok's scales as she whispered words of encouragement to him. "We can do this," she said softly.

Noah stood by her side, his eyes filled with determination. "We won't let them win."

With a surge of adrenaline, Sara and Noah's group charged forward, unleashing their elemental powers upon the unsuspecting poachers. The battle was fierce and chaotic, but their loyalty to each other and to the dragons fueled their strength.

In the end, victory was theirs. The poachers were defeated and driven away from their sanctuary lands. As Sara looked around at her friends and allies standing tall amidst the aftermath of battle, she felt an overwhelming sense of pride and gratitude.

"We did it," she whispered, her voice filled with awe.

Noah smiled at her, his eyes shining with newfound confidence. "And we'll continue to protect this magical world together."

As the sun began to set over the mountain town, casting a warm glow upon their weary faces, Sara and Noah knew that their journey was far from over.

But they also knew that as long as they stood united, they would face any danger that came their way.

And so, with hearts full of hope and determination, they prepared for the next chapter of their extraordinary adventure.

17

Chapter 4: Confronting Danger

1. Infiltrating the Poachers' Lair

Sara and Noah huddled together, their eyes fixed on the dilapidated cabin nestled deep within the dense forest. It was the poachers' lair, a place where innocent creatures were captured and enslaved for profit. Determined to gather evidence against these heartless criminals, they devised a plan to infiltrate their hideout.

"We have to be careful," Sara whispered, her voice filled with determination. "We need to navigate through traps and avoid detection."

Noah nodded nervously, his hands trembling slightly. "I-I'm scared, Sara.

What if we get caught?"

Sara placed a reassuring hand on her brother's shoulder. "Don't worry, Noah.

We're not alone in this. We have Zarok and our allies by our side."

With Zarok leading the way, they cautiously approached the cabin. The air was thick with tension as they tiptoed past tripwires and avoided creaky floorboards. Every step brought them closer to uncovering the truth behind the poaching operation.

Suddenly, a trapdoor swung open beneath their feet, sending them plummeting into darkness. They landed with a thud in an underground chamber filled with cages of captured creatures.

"Are you two alright?" came a familiar voice from one of the cages.

Sara's eyes widened in surprise as she recognized Luna, a majestic unicorn they had met during their training at the dragon preserve.

"Luna! What are you doing here?" Sara exclaimed.

Luna lowered her head sadly. "I was captured while trying to protect my herd from these poachers."

Noah's heart sank at Luna's words but he quickly regained his resolve. "We'll get you out of here, Luna."

Together, they worked tirelessly to free Luna and other magical creatures trapped in cages nearby. As they released each creature, a sense of unity and determination filled the air.

1. Unexpected Allies

As they continued their mission, Sara and Noah encountered unexpected allies within the poachers' lair. They stumbled upon a hidden chamber where other magical creatures were held captive or enslaved by the poachers.

Among them was Orion, a wise old phoenix with fiery feathers that glowed even in the dim light of the chamber. "You've come to rescue us," he said, his voice filled with gratitude.

Sara nodded, her eyes gleaming with determination. "We won't let these poachers harm any more innocent creatures."

With Orion's guidance, they formed a united front against their common enemy. The magical creatures shared their knowledge and abilities, strengthening Sara and Noah's resolve to put an end to this cruel operation.

Together, they devised a plan to confront the leader of the dragon poaching operation and free all captive creatures from harm.

1. Showdown with Sinister Forces

The time for confrontation had arrived. Sara, Noah, Zarok, Luna, Orion, and their newfound allies stood before the leader of the dragon poaching operation

- a menacing figure cloaked in darkness.

"You dare challenge me?" the leader sneered, his voice dripping with malice.

Sara stepped forward boldly. "We will not allow you to continue your wicked deeds!"

A thrilling battle ensued as Sara and her allies fought valiantly against the sinister forces that threatened their world. Zarok unleashed his fiery breath while Luna used her healing powers to protect her comrades. Orion soared through the air, engulfing their enemies in flames.

Noah summoned his courage and joined the fight alongside his sister.

Together, they proved that loyalty and friendship could overcome any obstacle.

In the midst of chaos and danger, Sara caught sight of something glimmering on the leader's neck - a pendant adorned with mysterious symbols similar to those carved into the glowing blue egg they had found in the hidden cave.

With a surge of determination, Sara lunged forward and snatched the pendant from the leader's grasp. As she held it tightly in her hand, a surge of power coursed through her veins.

The leader's eyes widened in disbelief as he realized his defeat was imminent. "You may have won this battle, but we will rise again," he hissed before disappearing into the shadows.

Sara and Noah stood triumphantly amidst their allies, their hearts filled with a sense of accomplishment. They had not only protected themselves but also freed countless creatures from harm.

As they made their way back to the dragon preserve, Sara and Noah couldn't help but reflect on their journey. They had learned that true strength came not only from within but also from the bonds they formed with others.

Little did they know that their adventures were far from over. The mystical dragon kingdom still needed their help, and together with Zarok, Luna, Orion, and their newfound allies, they would face even greater challenges in the battles yet to come.

And so, as they walked hand in hand towards an uncertain future, Sara and Noah knew that they were no longer outsiders but integral parts of a world where magic thrived and friendship prevailed.

22

Chapter 5: Triumph and Sacrifice

1. Victory at a Cost

Sara, Noah, Zarok, and their allies emerged from the battle against the sinister forces victorious but not unscathed. The air was heavy with both triumph and sorrow as they surveyed the aftermath of the fierce confrontation. The dragon sanctuary had suffered significant damage, and some of their brave allies had made the ultimate sacrifice for the greater good.

Sara's heart ached as she thought of those they had lost along the way.

Their sacrifices weighed heavily on her mind, reminding her of the true cost of their mission. She couldn't help but feel a sense of guilt mixed with gratitude for those who had given everything to protect their world.

Noah stood beside her, his usually shy demeanor replaced by a solemn determination. He too understood the price that had been paid for their victory. His eyes glistened with unshed tears as he silently mourned the fallen heroes who had become like family to them.

Zarok, their loyal dragon companion, sensed their grief and nudged them gently with his snout. "We have won this battle," he said softly into their minds, his voice filled with both relief and sadness. "But we must honor those who have fallen by continuing to fight for our cause."

Sara nodded, wiping away a tear that escaped down her cheek. "You're right, Zarok," she replied, her voice steady despite her emotions. "We can't let their sacrifices be in vain."

Together, they turned towards their remaining allies – humans and dragons alike – who were also grappling with loss. They shared stories of bravery and heroism, finding solace in each other's support. In these moments of shared grief, they discovered strength they never knew they possessed.

1. Healing Wounds

In the days that followed, Sara, Noah, Zarok, and their remaining allies took time to mourn their losses and heal their wounds. The dragon sanctuary became a place of solace and reflection, where they could find peace amidst the chaos that had unfolded.

Sara found comfort in the presence of her friends, both human and dragon. They shared memories of their fallen comrades, celebrating their lives and the impact they had made. Through tears and laughter, they honored the sacrifices that had been made and found strength in each other's support.

Noah, too, found solace in the company of his newfound friends. They listened patiently as he spoke about his fears and insecurities, offering words of encouragement and understanding. Together, they helped him navigate through his grief, reminding him that he was not alone.

As they reflected on their journey thus far, Sara realized how much she had grown throughout their adventures. She had learned the true meaning of loyalty and friendship – lessons that could only be taught through sacrifice and loss. She vowed to carry these lessons with her always, cherishing the memories of those who had fought alongside them.

1. Rebuilding and Moving Forward

With their wounds healing and their spirits renewed, Sara, Noah, Zarok, and their allies turned their attention towards rebuilding the damaged parts of the dragon sanctuary. They worked tirelessly to restore what had been lost, ensuring its future protection for generations to come.

The once-broken walls were mended with care, while new enchantments were placed to strengthen its defenses against future threats. Humans and dragons worked side by side in harmony – a testament to the bond they had formed throughout their journey.

As plans for a brighter future took shape, Sara couldn't help but feel a sense of hope wash over her. The sanctuary would thrive once again as a safe haven for dragons and humans alike. It would serve as a reminder of what they had fought for – a world where magical creatures could live in peace alongside humans.

Zarok soared through the sky, his wings beating with a newfound sense of freedom. He circled above the sanctuary, his eyes filled with pride and gratitude for all they had accomplished. The sacrifices made along the way had not been in vain – they had paved the way for a future where dragons could flourish.

Sara, Noah, Zarok, and their allies stood together, gazing at the sanctuary they had rebuilt. They knew that their journey was far from over, but they were ready to face whatever challenges lay ahead. With hearts full of determination and minds filled with newfound wisdom, they embarked on the next chapter of their adventure – united in their mission to protect and preserve their magical world.

And so, as the sun set on another day in the remote mountain town, Sara and Noah felt a sense of triumph and sacrifice intertwine within them. They were no longer outsiders; they were warriors fighting for a cause greater than themselves. And together, with their dragon companion by their side, they would continue to shape their destiny and create a future where magic thrived.

52

27

Chapter 6: A New Chapter Begins

1. Epilogue: A Glimpse of the Future

The sun began to set over the mountain town, casting a warm golden glow across the landscape. Sara and Noah stood on their porch, gazing out at the breathtaking view before them. It had been months since they had discovered Zarok, the baby dragon who had changed their lives forever.

As they watched the dragons soaring through the sky, Sara couldn't help but feel a sense of awe and wonder. The once-remote mountain town had transformed into a bustling community where dragons and humans coexisted harmoniously. The bond between these magical creatures and their human allies had grown stronger with each passing day.

Noah turned to his sister with a smile on his face. "Remember when we first found Zarok? We never could have imagined all of this."

Sara nodded, her heart filled with gratitude for the incredible journey they had embarked upon. "I'm so grateful for everything we've experienced together," she said softly. "We've made lifelong friends and learned so much about ourselves and the world around us."

1. Reflections and Gratitude

As night fell, Sara, Noah, Zarok, and their remaining allies gathered around a crackling fire in the heart of the dragon preserve. The wizard guardians shared stories of their own adventures and expressed their gratitude for Sara and Noah's bravery.

"I remember when I first met you two," said Merlin, one of the oldest wizards in the sanctuary. "You were just children then, but you showed such courage in standing up against those who sought to harm our world."

Sara blushed at Merlin's words but couldn't help feeling proud of how far they had come. She looked around at her friends - both human and dragon - who had become like family to her.

"We couldn't have done any of this without all of you," Sara said, her voice filled with emotion. "You believed in us and taught us so much. We will forever be grateful."

Noah nodded in agreement, his eyes shining with gratitude. "Thank you for showing us a world of magic and friendship," he said softly.

1. The End... or is it?

As the fire crackled and the night grew darker, a sense of anticipation hung in the air. The dragons circled overhead, their wings creating a gentle breeze that rustled through the trees.

Zarok nudged Sara and Noah, his eyes gleaming with excitement. "This may be the end of one chapter, but it's just the beginning of another," he said, his voice echoing in their minds.

Sara looked at Zarok curiously. "What do you mean?"

The baby dragon smiled mischievously. "There are still many adventures waiting for us out there," he replied. "New challenges to face, new friendships to forge."

Noah's eyes widened with excitement as he realized what Zarok was hinting at. "You mean... there could be more dragons out there? More hidden sanctuaries?"

Zarok nodded, his scales shimmering in the moonlight. "Indeed," he said. "Our journey has only just begun."

Sara and Noah exchanged glances, their hearts filled with hope and anticipation for what lay ahead. They knew that their bond with Zarok would guide them through whatever challenges they may face.

As they looked up at the starry sky, they couldn't help but feel a sense of wonder and possibility. The adventure may have come to an end for now, but a new chapter had just begun.

And so, as the night stretched on and the dragons soared above them, Sara, Noah, Zarok, and their friends embraced the unknown future that awaited them.

The End... or is it?

31

Sara and her family move to a remote mountain town, where she feels like an outsider at her new school. While exploring the woods behind their house, Sara and her brother Noah discover a hidden cave with a glowing blue egg inside. The egg hatches into a baby dragon named Zarok, who forms an empathetic bond with both of them.

Zarok reveals that he is from a dragon kingdom that was driven into hiding by dragon hunters. He needs Sara and Noah's help to find his tribe. They follow Zarok up the mountain to a cloud-cloaked preserve where dragons secretly live alongside wizard guardians. There, they learn about their endangered magical world and train in elemental dragon riding skills.

As news spreads of a dangerous dragon poaching threat, Sara and Noah join forces with other magical creatures, human allies, and young dragon riders to protect the preservation lands. They face daring risks and learn the true meaning of loyalty and friendship.

The climax of the story comes when the group faces their biggest challenge yet in confronting the sinister forces threatening the dragons' sanctuary. The resolution offers a glimpse of the outcome without revealing all the details, leaving some mystery for readers to discover.

Overall, "The Lost Dragon Riders" is an exciting adventure filled with magic, friendship, and bravery as Sara and Noah embark on a journey to save the dragons and their world from danger.